HOW TO DRAW FIVE NIGHTS AT FREDDY'S

EASY AND FUN
STEP-BY-STEP DRAWING

Mangle

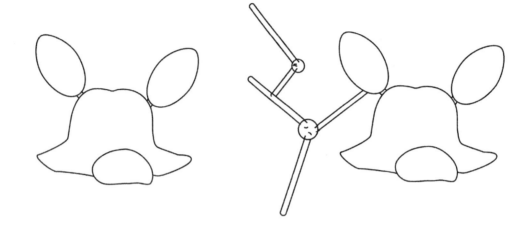

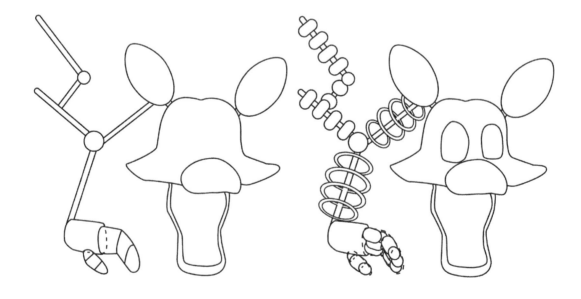

PRACTICE PAGE

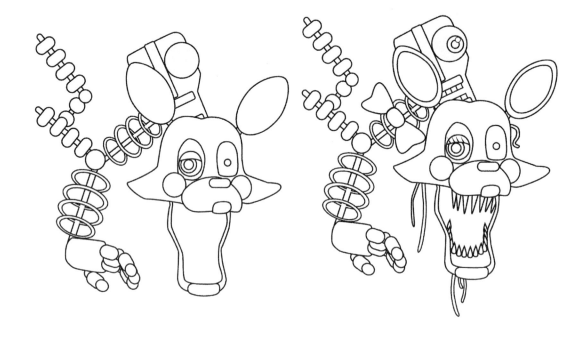

PRACTICE PAGE

Foxy

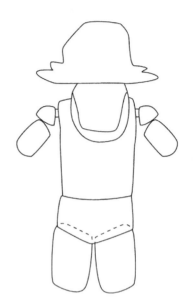
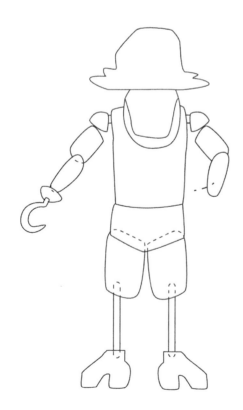
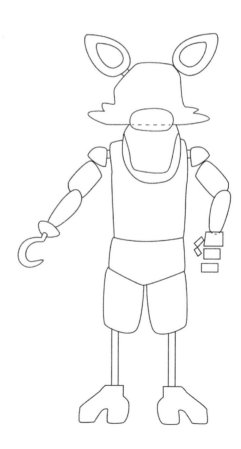

PRACTICE PAGE

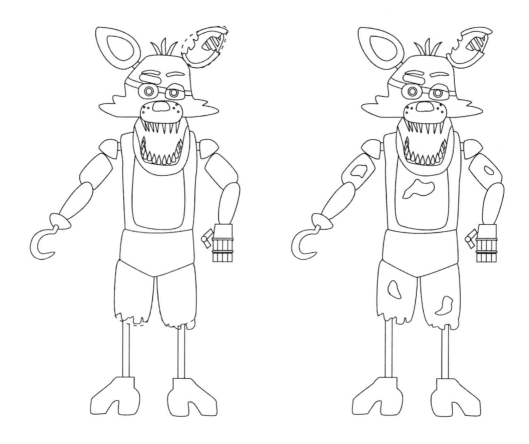

PRACTICE PAGE

Nightmare Chika

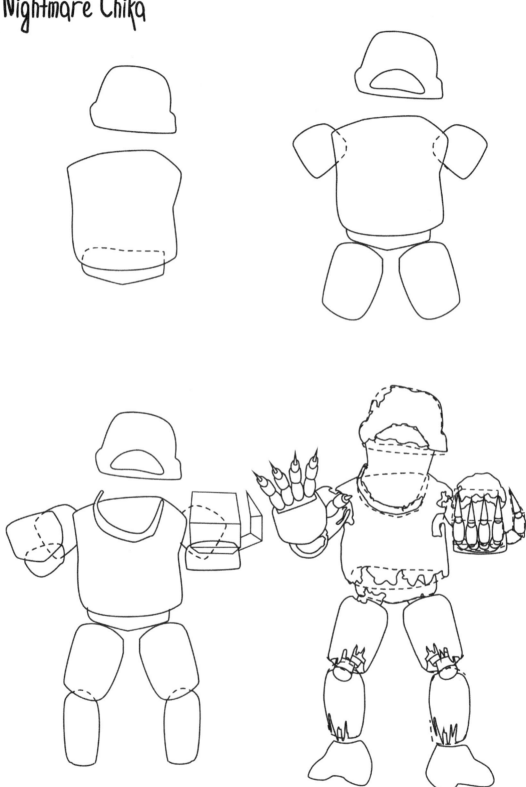

PRACTICE PAGE

PRACTICE PAGE

Nightmare Baloon Boy

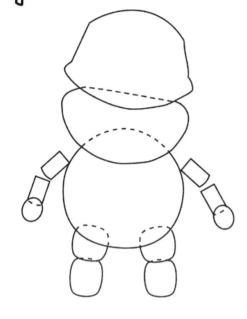

PRACTICE PAGE

Nightmare Foxy

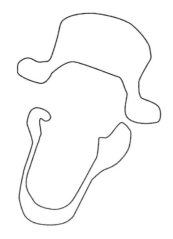

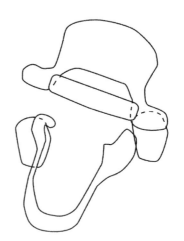

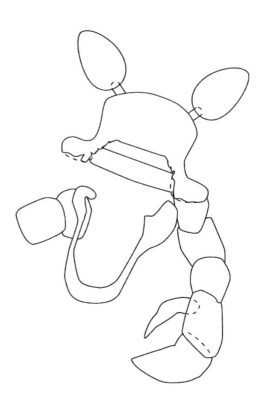

PRACTICE PAGE

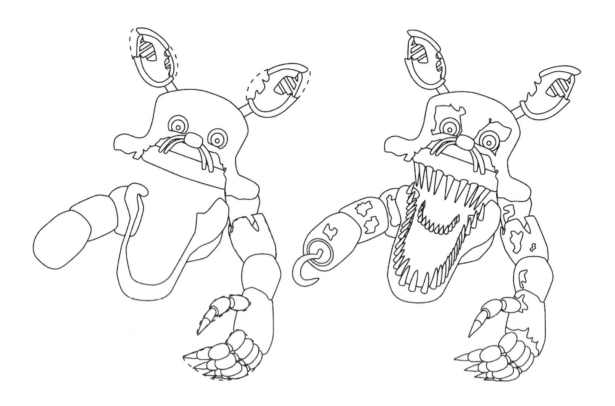

PRACTICE PAGE

Baloon Boy

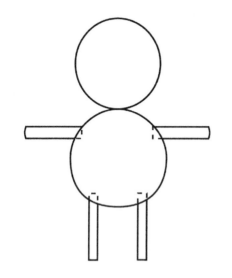

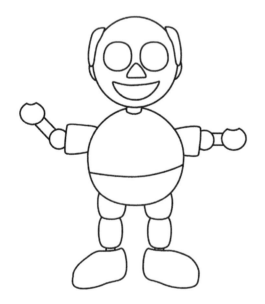

PRACTICE PAGE

PRACTICE PAGE

PRACTICE PAGE

Plushtrap

PRACTICE PAGE

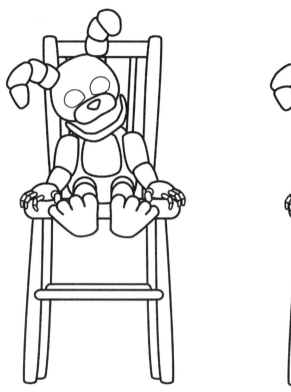

PRACTICE PAGE

Bidybab

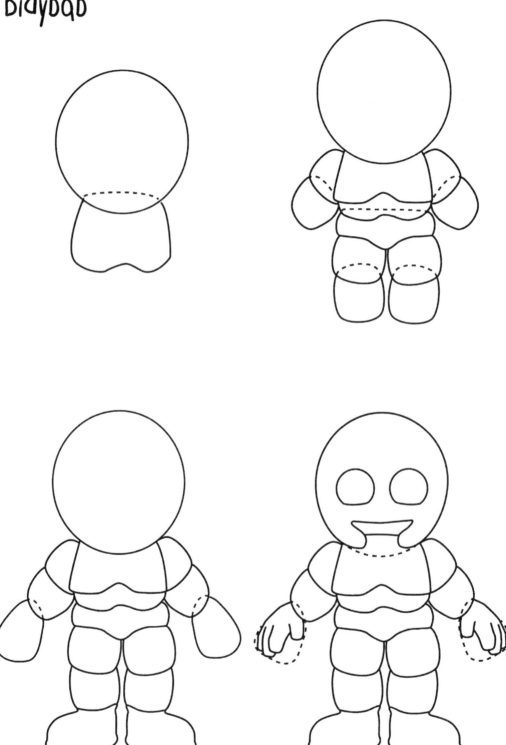

PRACTICE PAGE

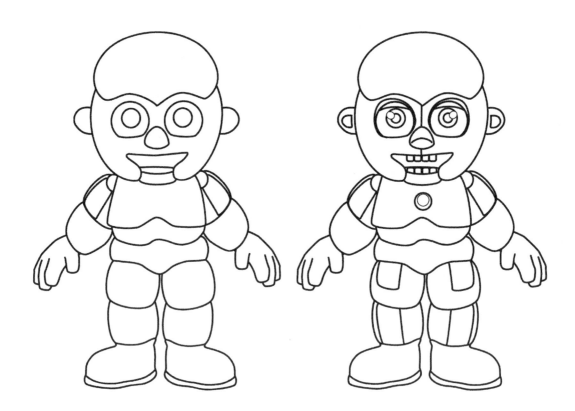

PRACTICE PAGE

Funtime Freddy

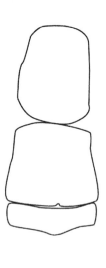
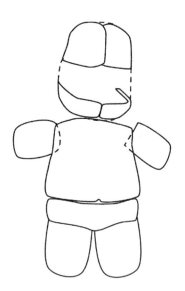
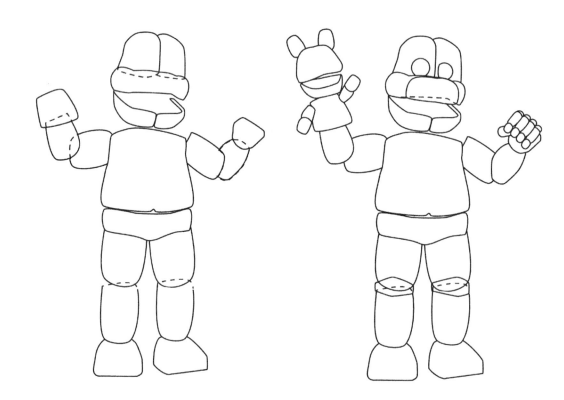

PRACTICE PAGE

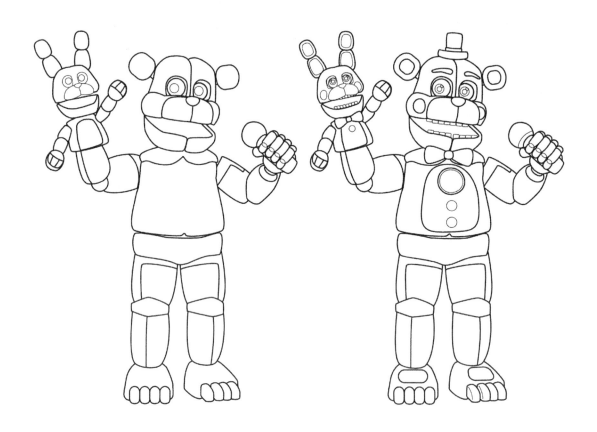

PRACTICE PAGE

Ballora

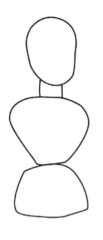
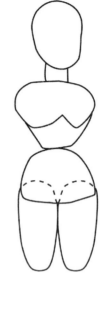

PRACTICE PAGE

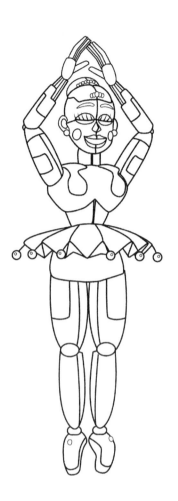

PRACTICE PAGE

Nightmarionne

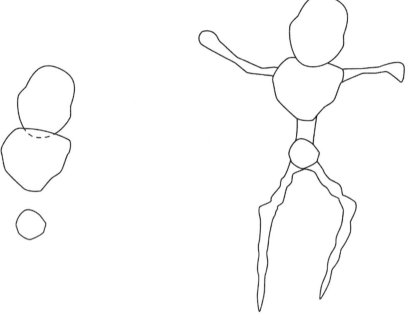

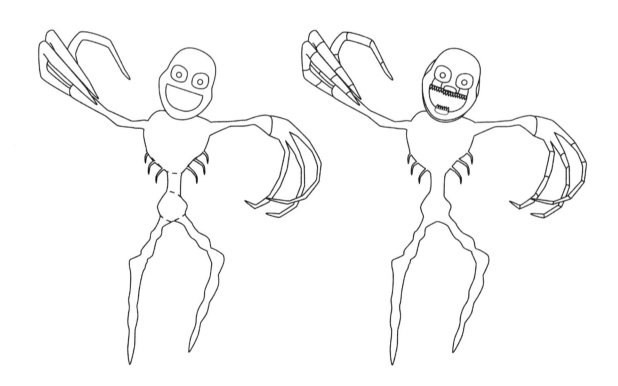

PRACTICE PAGE

Jack-O-Bonnie

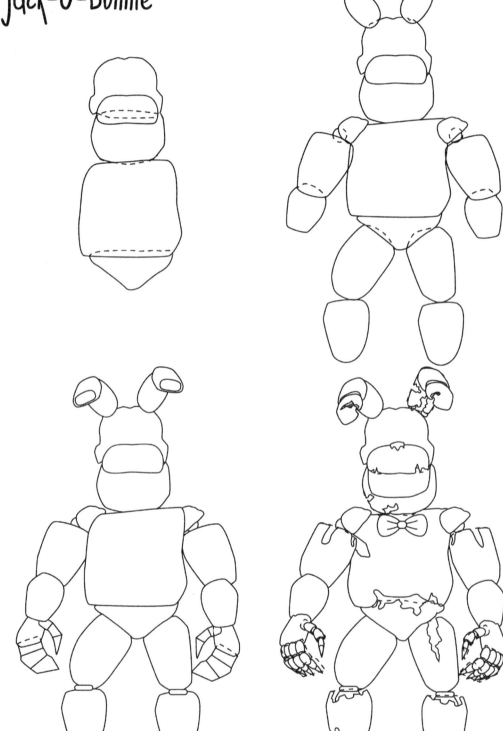

PRACTICE PAGE

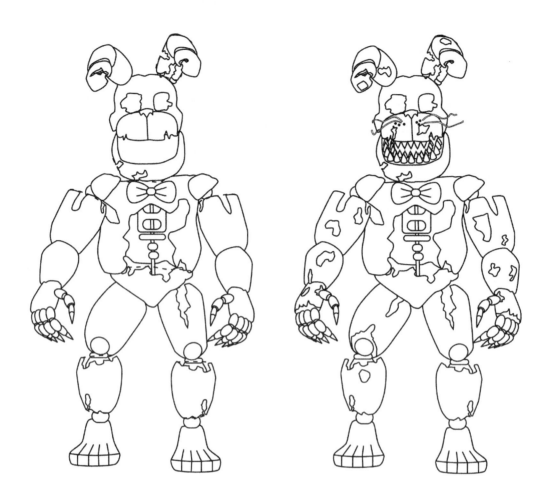

PRACTICE PAGE

Ennard

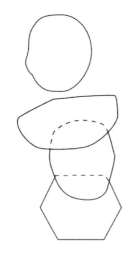 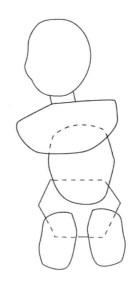

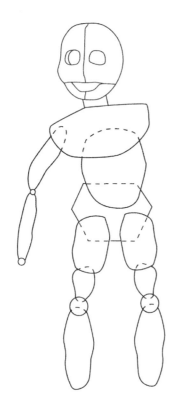 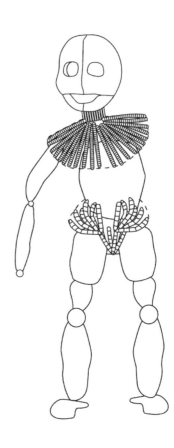

PRACTICE PAGE

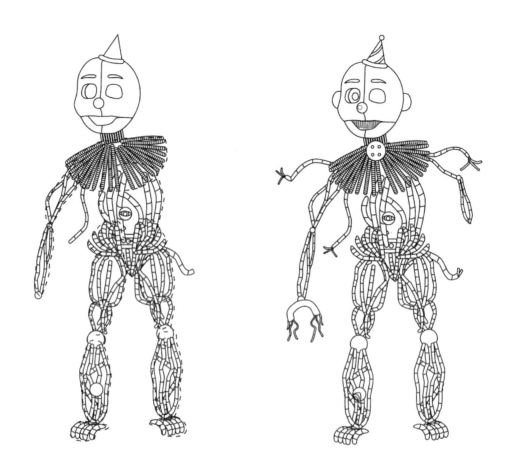

PRACTICE PAGE

Twisted Foxy

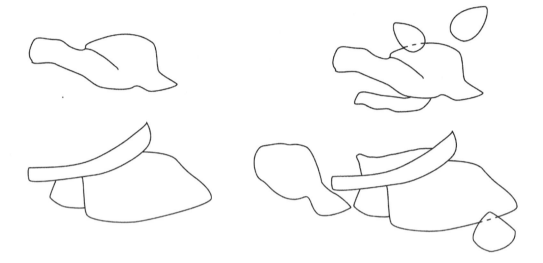

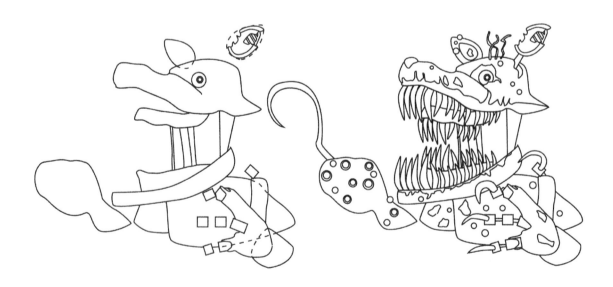

PRACTICE PAGE

Twisted Bonnie

PRACTICE PAGE

Jack-O-Chica

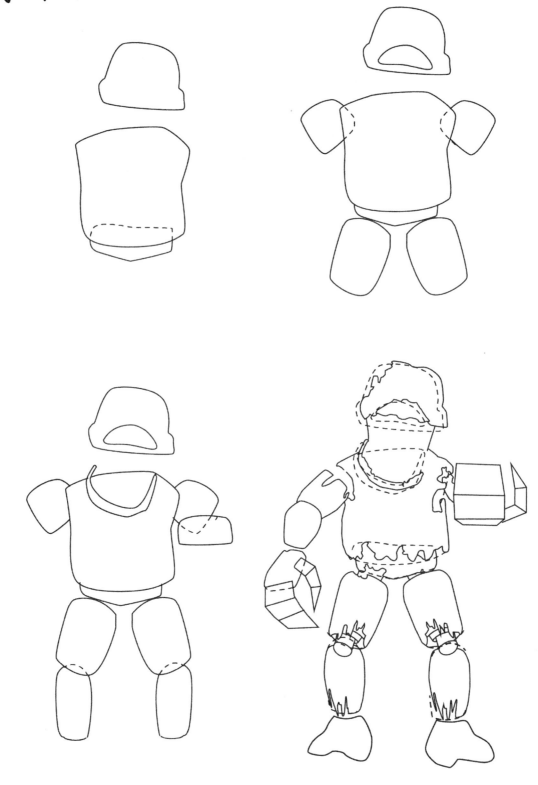

PRACTICE PAGE

PRACTICE PAGE

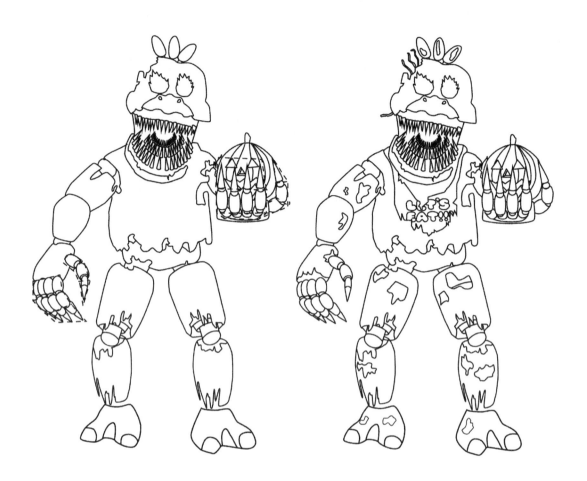

PRACTICE PAGE

Twisted Freddy

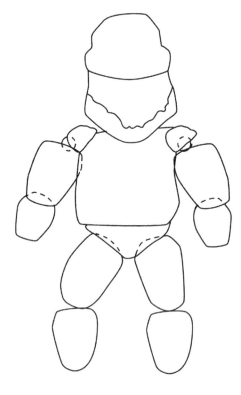

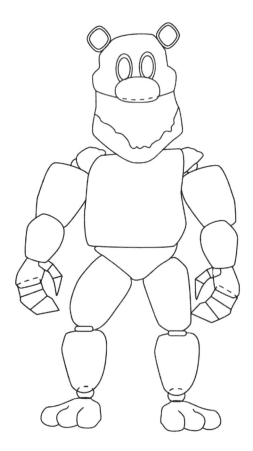

PRACTICE PAGE

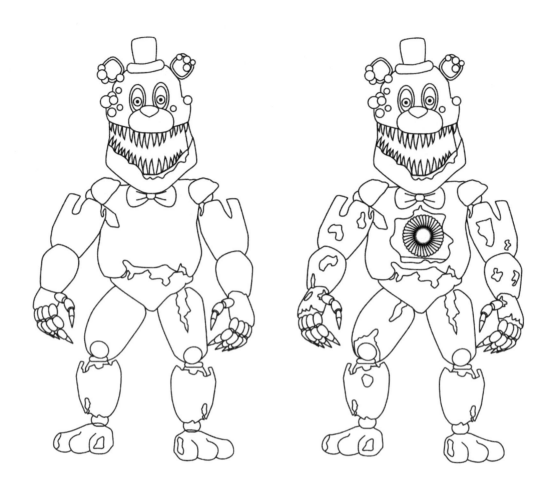

PRACTICE PAGE

Minireena

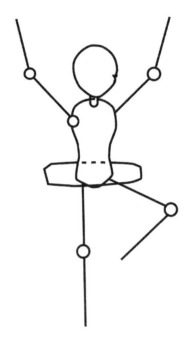

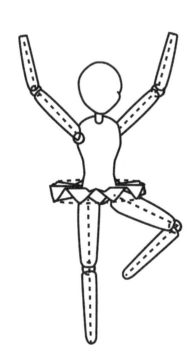

PRACTICE PAGE

Circus Baby

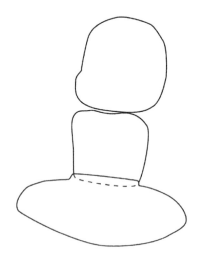 

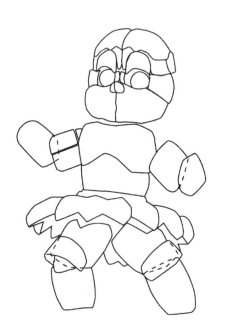 

PRACTICE PAGE

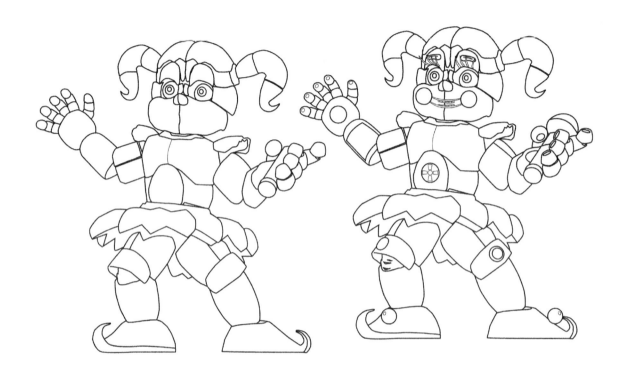

PRACTICE PAGE

Paperpals

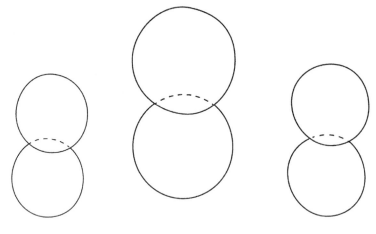

PRACTICE PAGE

PRACTICE PAGE

Chica

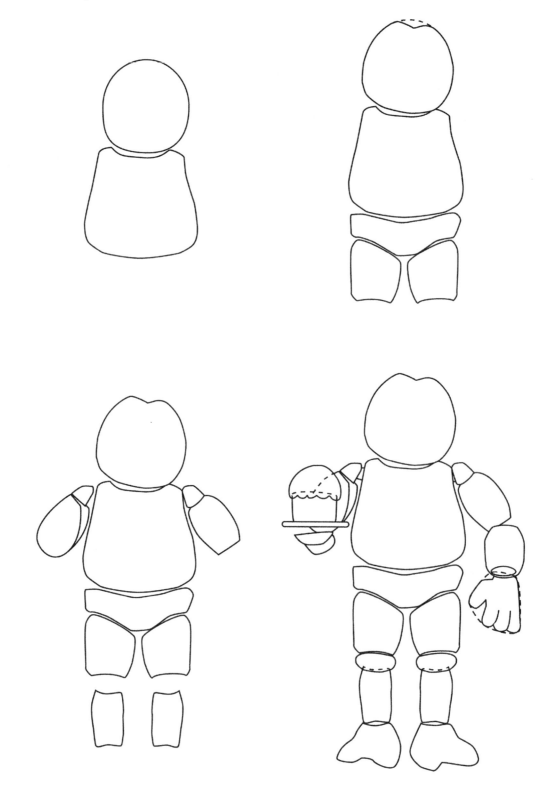

PRACTICE PAGE

PRACTICE PAGE

Springtrap

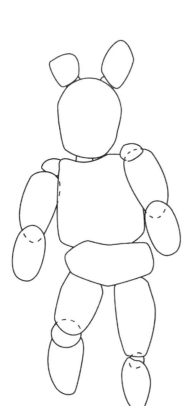

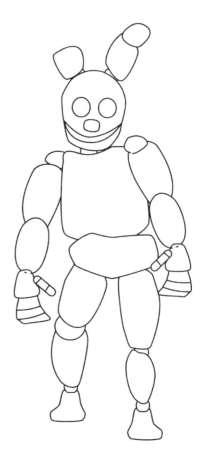

PRACTICE PAGE

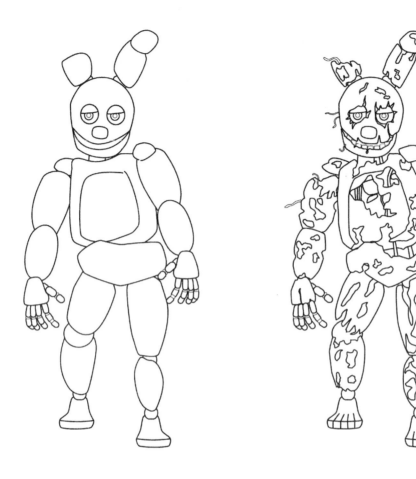

PRACTICE PAGE

Endo 02

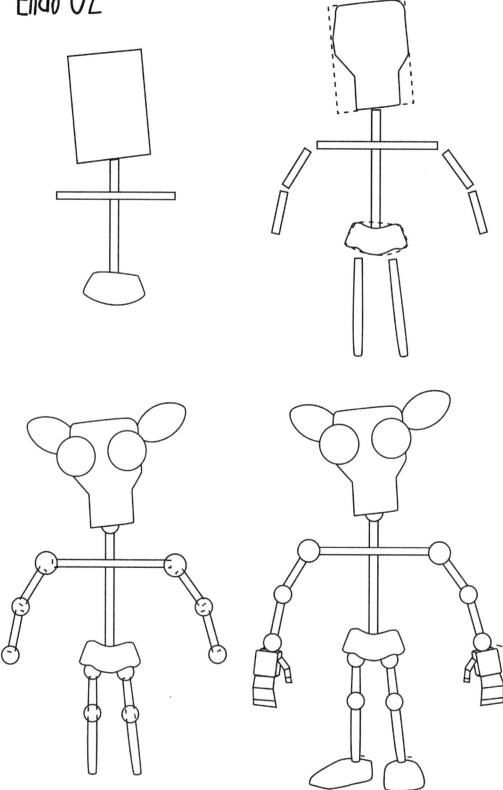

PRACTICE PAGE

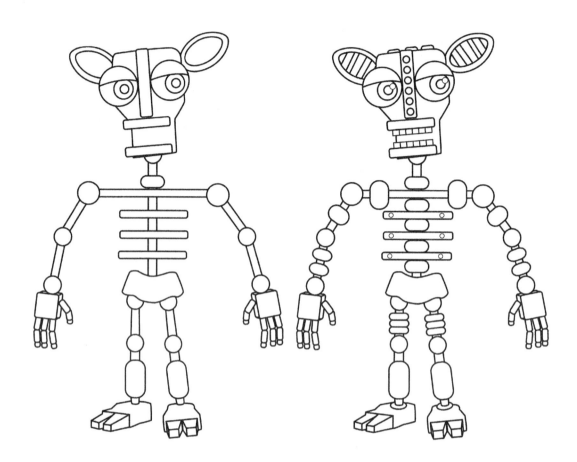

PRACTICE PAGE

Golden Freddy

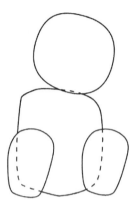 

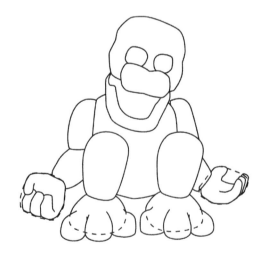 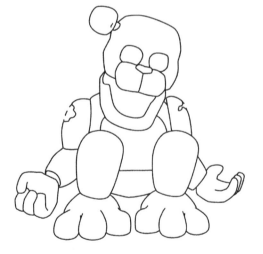

PRACTICE PAGE

PRACTICE PAGE

Twisted Chica

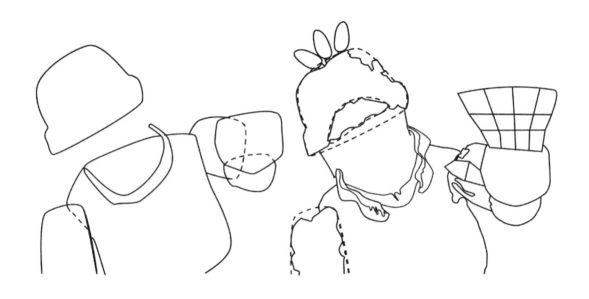

PRACTICE PAGE

Freddy

PRACTICE PAGE

PRACTICE PAGE

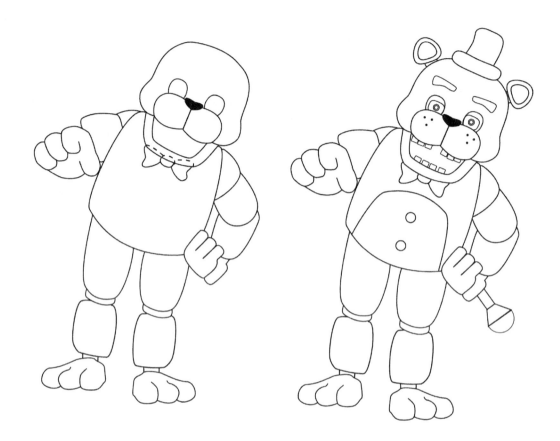

PRACTICE PAGE

Bonnie

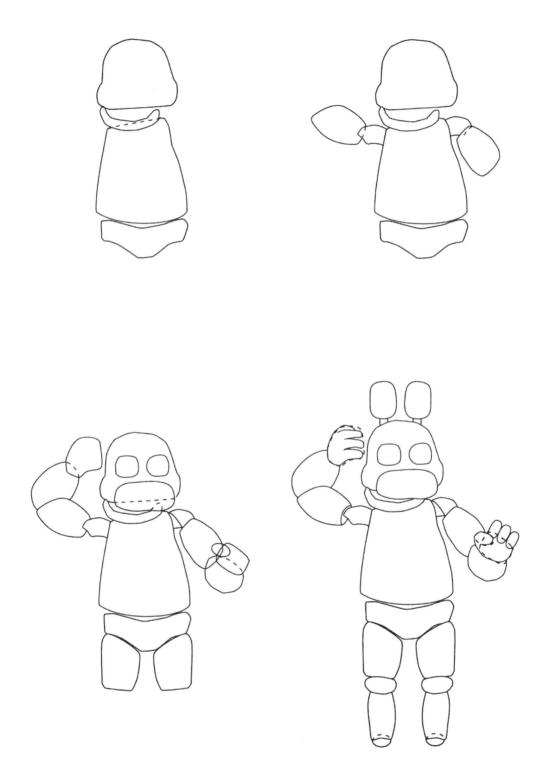

PRACTICE PAGE

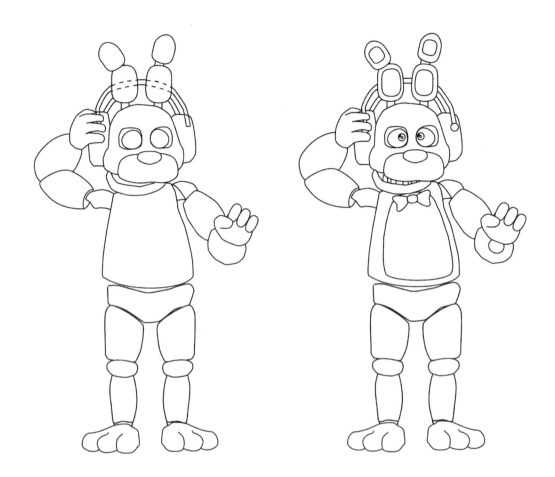

PRACTICE PAGE

Nightmare Freddy

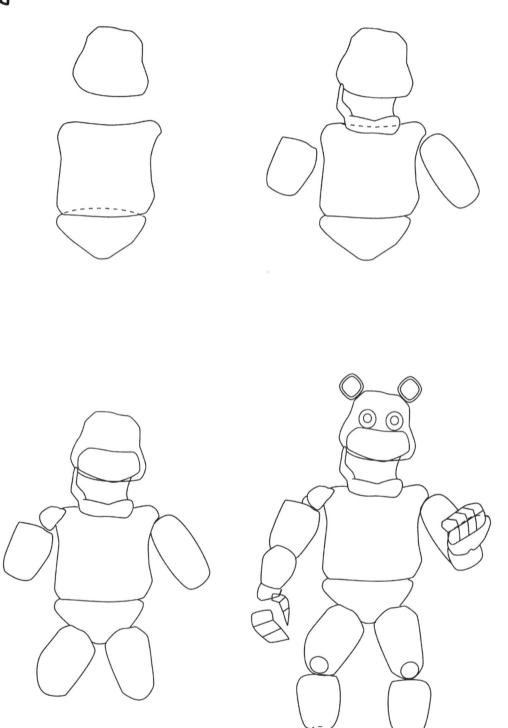

PRACTICE PAGE

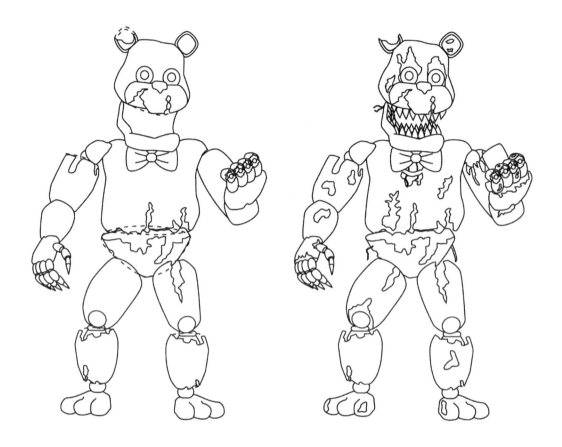

PRACTICE PAGE

Nightmare Bonnie

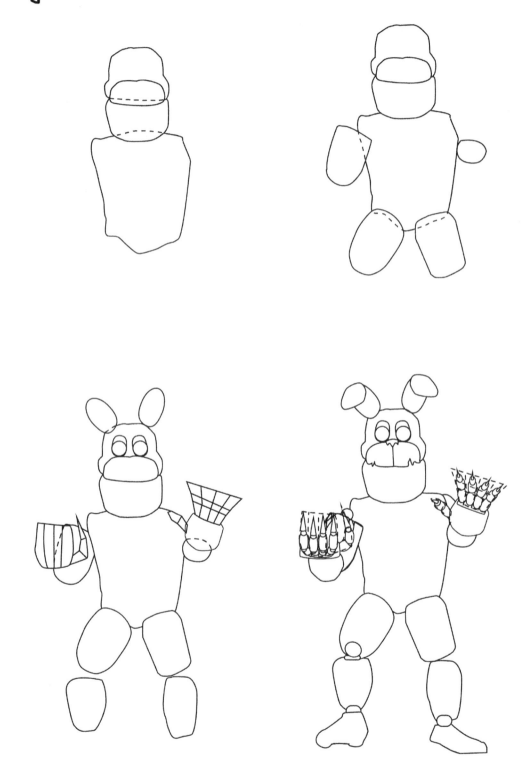

PRACTICE PAGE

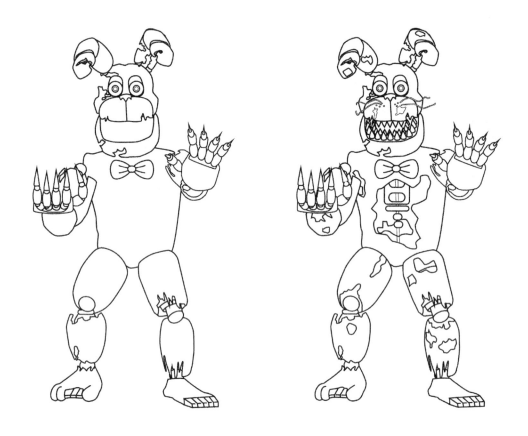

PRACTICE PAGE

Endo 01

PRACTICE PAGE

PRACTICE PAGE

Printed in Great Britain
by Amazon